AF605704

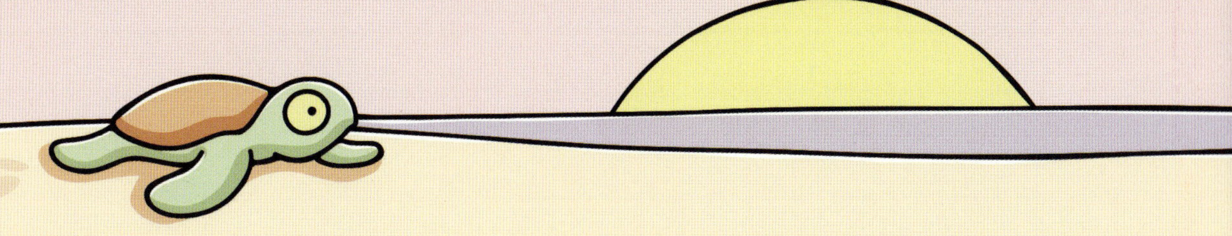

First published by Affirm Press in 2024
Bunurong/Boon Wurrung Country
28 Thistlethwaite Street,
South Melbourne, VIC 3205
affirmpress.com.au

1 3 5 7 9 10 8 6 4 2

Affirm Press is located on the unceded land of the Bunurong/Boon Wurrung peoples of the Kulin Nation. Affirm Press pays respect to their Elders past and present.

A catalogue record for this book is available from the National Library of Australia

ISBN: 9781923046610 (hardback)
Cover and internal design by Brent Turner © Affirm Press
Printed and bound in China by RR Donnelley Asia Printing Solutions Ltd.

MIX
Paper | Supporting responsible forestry
FSC® C144853

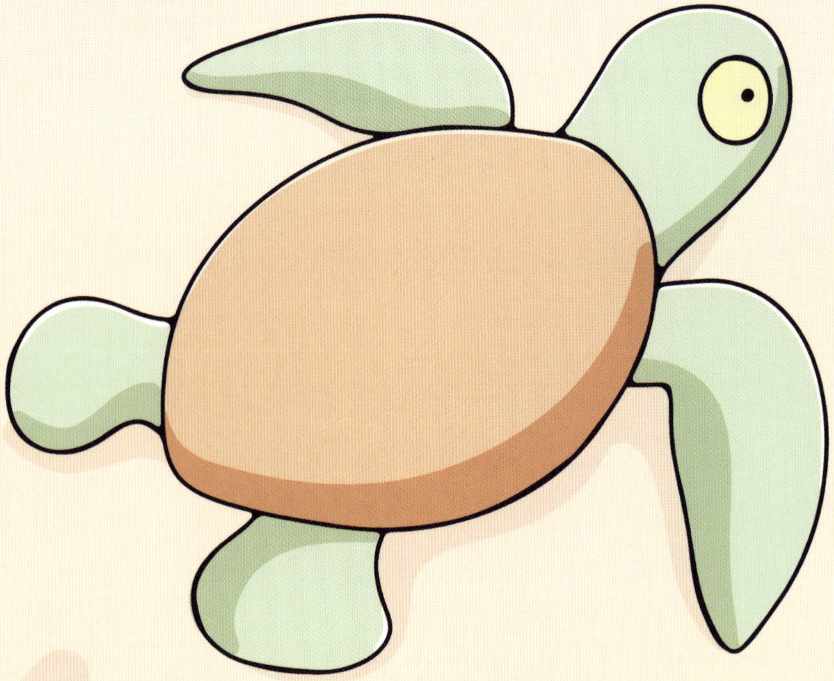

WIRES is Australia's largest wildlife rescue organisation and has been rescuing and caring for sick, injured and orphaned native animals for 35 years. WIRES's mission is to actively rehabilitate and preserve Australian wildlife and inspire others to do the same.
Find out more at wires.org.au.
By purchasing this book you are supporting WIRES. Affirm Press donates 3% of gross profits and Brentos donates 3% of royalty earnings.

We respect and honour the connection of Traditional Owners with their sacred lands and seas. Australia's marine and national parks exist because of this rich history and stewardship.

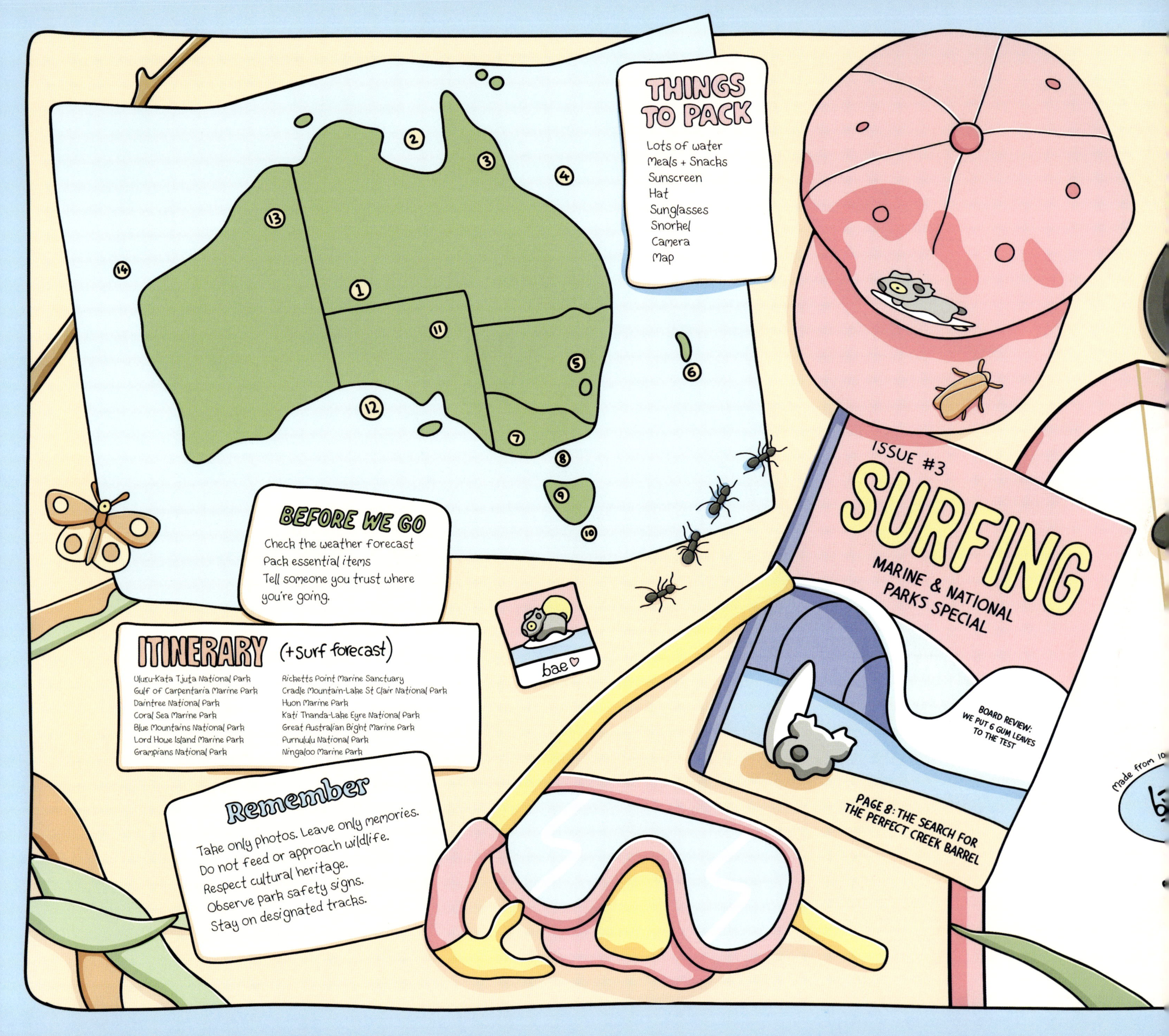

THINGS TO PACK
Lots of water
Meals + Snacks
Sunscreen
Hat
Sunglasses
Snorkel
Camera
Map
BEFORE WE GO
Check the weather forecast
Pack essential items
Tell someone you trust where you're going.
ITINERARY (+Surf forecast)
Uluṟu-Kata Tjuṯa National Park
Gulf of Carpentaria Marine Park
Daintree National Park
Coral Sea Marine Park
Blue Mountains National Park
Lord Howe Island Marine Park
Grampians National Park
Ricketts Point Marine Sanctuary
Cradle Mountain-Lake St Clair National Park
Huon Marine Park
Kati Thanda-Lake Eyre National Park
Great Australian Bight Marine Park
Purnululu National Park
Ningaloo Marine Park
Remember
Take only photos. Leave only memories.
Do not feed or approach wildlife.
Respect cultural heritage.
Observe park safety signs.
Stay on designated tracks.
bae♡
ISSUE #3
SURFING
MARINE & NATIONAL PARKS SPECIAL
BOARD REVIEW: WE PUT 6 GUM LEAVES TO THE TEST
PAGE 8: THE SEARCH FOR THE PERFECT CREEK BARREL

PACK YOUR BAGS FOR AN ADVENTURE INTO AUSTRALIA'S WILD WONDERS.

Australia's marine and national parks are vital sanctuaries that conserve unique ecosystems, safeguard endangered species, protect our rich Indigenous heritage and provide us with incredible places to play, relax and connect with nature.

From pristine coral reefs to ancient forests, every park has a history and purpose. So, grab your backpack and let's take a journey into the wild places that make Australia so special.

Waterfalls stream down the red face of Uluṟu after heavy rain. Did you know Uluṟu stands at 348 metres above the desert? That's taller than the Sydney Opera House and Harbour Bridge combined!

DANCE WITH NATURE
WELCOME TO
Uluru-Kata Tjuta
NATIONAL PARK
Welcome to Aboriginal Land
NORTHERN TERRITORY
1,325 SQUARE KILOMETRES
ANANGU COUNTRY
LOOK OUT FOR WILDLIFE
Emu
Thorny Devil
King Brown Snake
Greater Bilby
Dingo

Gulf Of Carpentaria
MARINE PARK
The sea lives in all of us
THE WELLESLEY ISLAND SEA CLAIM AND THUWATHA/ BUJIMULLA INDIGENOUS PROTECTED AREAS OVERLAP WITH THE MARINE PARK
Northern Territory
70 METRES MAX. DEPTH
23,771 SQUARE KILOMETRES
Look out for sea life
Reef Shark
Hawksbill Turtle
Olive Sea Snake
Dugong

Endangered sea turtles glide peacefully through coral reefs and undersea pinnacles. Did you know these protected habitats provide a home to other vulnerable creatures like sharks, Dugongs and sea snakes?

The low rumble of Cassowaries filter
through the treetops of the Daintree
Rainforest. Did you know it's the oldest
surviving tropical rainforest in the world?
It's over 135 million years old!

Daintree
National Park
1,200 SQUARE KILOMETRES
QUEENSLAND
Eastern
Kuku Yalanji
Country
BEWARE
LOOK OUT FOR WILDLIFE
Short-Beaked
Echidna
Rainbow
Bee-Eater
Striped
Possum
Boyd's Forest
Dragon

WELCOME TO
CORAL SEA
MARINE PARK
ABORIGINAL AND
TORRES STRAIT ISLANDER
SEA COUNTRY
989,836
SQUARE
KILOMETRES
Look Out For Sea Life
Green Turtle
Manta Ray
Bottlenose Dolphin
QUEENSLAND
Seas the day

The Coral Sea Marine Park contains forested islands, coral reefs, deep sea canyons and 46 other unique habitats. Did you know six of the world's seven sea turtle species call these habitats home?

A flock of cockatoos descend upon the Three Sisters in the Blue Mountains National Park. Did you know that the Blue Mountains are home to the Tiger Quoll, which is the largest carnivorous marsupial in mainland Australia?

BLUE MOUNTAINS
National Park
2,680
SQUARE
KILOMETRES
Please don't feed wildlife
BLUE MOUNTAINS
i
RESPECT THE LOCALS
NEW SOUTH WALES
Ngurra
Country
LOOK OUT FOR WILDLIFE
Eastern Grey Kangaroo
Sulphur-Crested Cockatoo
Brushtail Possum

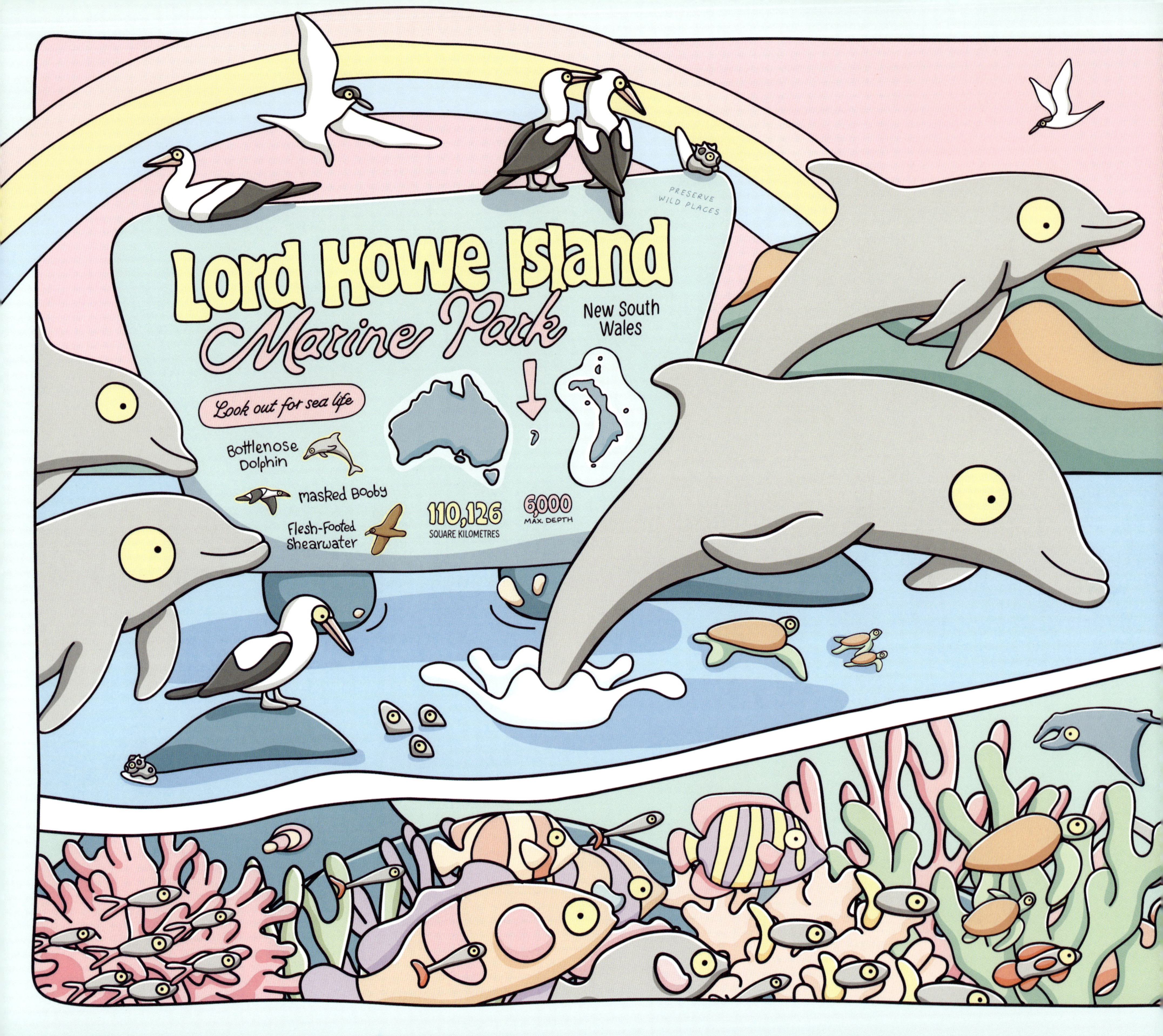
PRESERVE WILD PLACES
Lord Howe Island
Marine Park
New South Wales
Look out for sea life
Bottlenose Dolphin
masked Booby
Flesh-Footed Shearwater
110,126
SQUARE KILOMETRES
6,000
MAX. DEPTH

Dolphins play in the coral reef lagoon of Lord Howe Island. Did you know this island is an extinct volcano that now provides homes for vulnerable seabirds and marine creatures?

A Koala and her joey explore a valley in the Grampians National Park, a place with 22,000 years of cultural heritage. Did you know it is home to the largest collection of Aboriginal rock art paintings in southern Australia?

WELCOME TO
GRAMPIANS
National Park
1,672
SQUARE
KILOMETRES
(Gariwerd)
Victoria
Djab Wurrung
and Jardwadjali
Country
LOOK OUT FOR WILDLIFE
Koala
Laughing
Kookaburra
Short-Beaked
Echidna
Take Only Memories.
Leave Only Footprints.

Welcome To
RICKETTS POINT
MARINE SANCTUARY
Take Only Photos
Tread Lightly
BEWARE
Blue-Ringed Octopus
1.15
SQUARE KILOMETRES
Victoria
BUNURONG SEA COUNTRY
LOOK OUT FOR SEA LIFE
Leafy Sea Dragon
Giant Cuttlefish
Yellow Leatherjacket
Pygmy Seahorse

Australian Pelicans gather around the rock pools of Ricketts Point Marine Sanctuary. Did you know these intertidal rock platforms are nurseries for unique sea and plant life?

Cradle Mountain is known for its diverse
landscapes including ancient rainforests,
snow-covered mountains and glacial lakes.
Did you know it's home to the endangered
Tasmanian Devil?

WELCOME TO
CRADLE MOUNTAIN-
LAKE ST CLAIR
National Park
THERE'S BLISS IN THE WILDERNESS
TASMANIA
1,614 SQUARE KILOMETRES
FIRST NATIONS COUNTRY
LOOK OUT FOR WILDLIFE
Platypus
Bare-Nosed Wombat
Green Rosella
Forester Kangaroo

HUON
Marine Park
Preserve natural habitats
9,991
SQUARE KILOMETRES
MELUKERDEE AND LYLUEQUONNY PEOPLES
TASMANIA
LOOK OUT FOR DEEP SEA LIFE
3,000
metres
MAX DEPTH
Giant Squid
Anglerfish
Oarfish

Did you know that there are more than 120 undersea mountains in Huon Marine Park, providing habitats for many marine species found nowhere else on Earth? The peaks of some of these 'seamounts' are 1,000 metres below the surface!

Did you know that Kati Thandra-Lake Eyre is Australia's largest salt lake? After flooding, the lake attracts millions of breeding water birds and can turn pink from salt-loving bacteria.

KATI THANDA-
LAKE EYRE
National Park
South Australia
ARABANA COUNTRY
BIRDS ARE MAGICAL
9,500 SQUARE KILOMETRES
LOOK OUT FOR WILDLIFE
Red-Necked Avocet
Curlew Sandpiper
Major Mitchell's Cockatoo
Galah

Great Australian Bight
Marine Park
45,822 SQUARE KILOMETRES
South Australia
EMBRACE NATURE
BEWARE
Sharks
6,000 metres MAX. DEPTH
MIRNING AND WIRANGU SEA COUNTRY
Great White Shark
Australian Fur Seal
Southern Right Whale
LOOK OUT FOR MARINE LIFE

The Great Australian Bight Marine Park protects endangered Southern Right Whales, who shelter here in winter to give birth. Did you know baby whales are called calves?

Purnululu National Park is home to the
Bungle Bungle Ranges. Did you know these
beehive-shaped domes tower 250 metres above
the savanna and provide important habitats
for wildlife and insects?

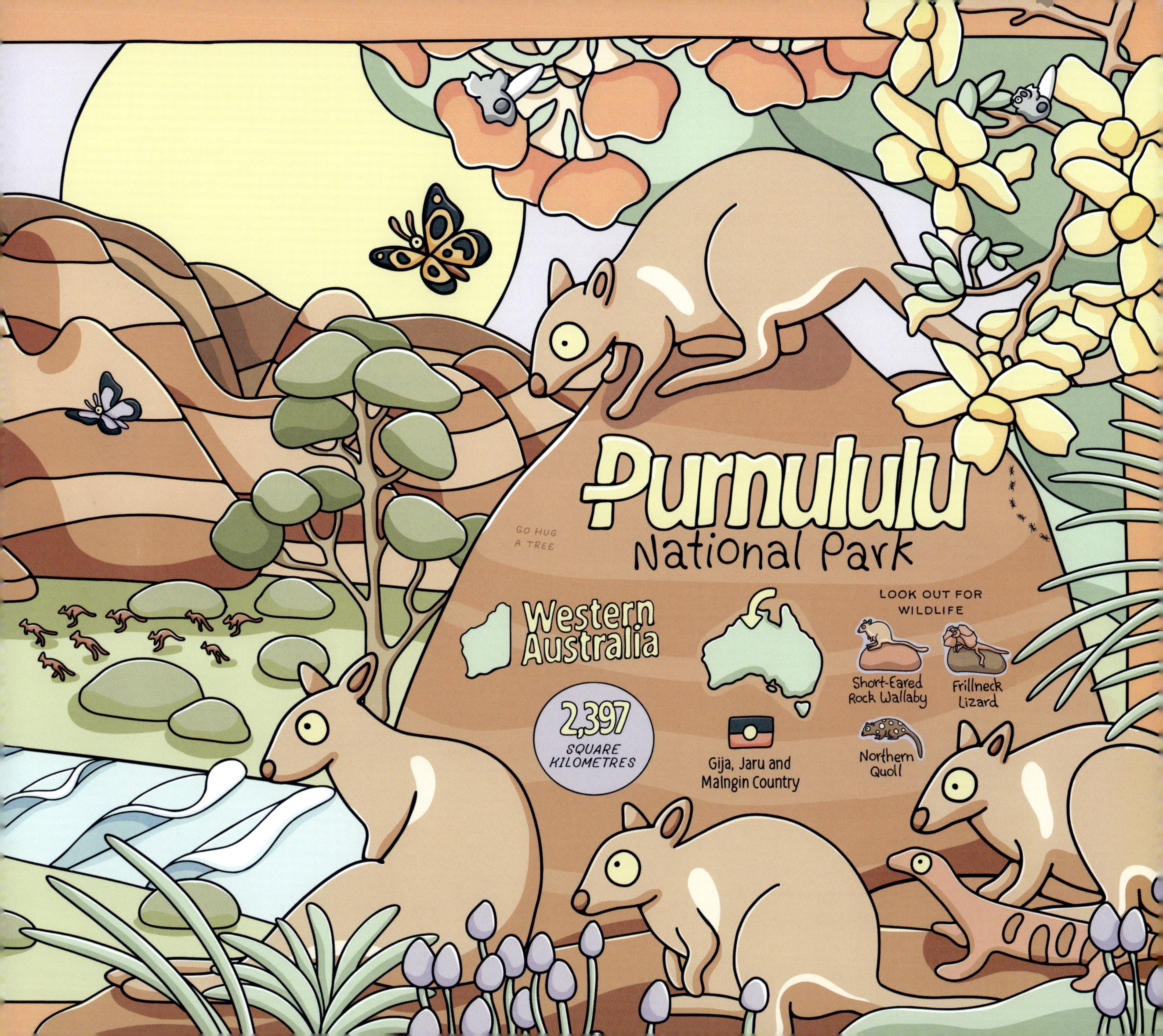

Purnululu
National Park
GO HUG A TREE
Western Australia
LOOK OUT FOR WILDLIFE
Short-Eared Rock Wallaby
Frillneck Lizard
Northern Quoll
2,397
SQUARE KILOMETRES
Gija, Jaru and Malngin Country

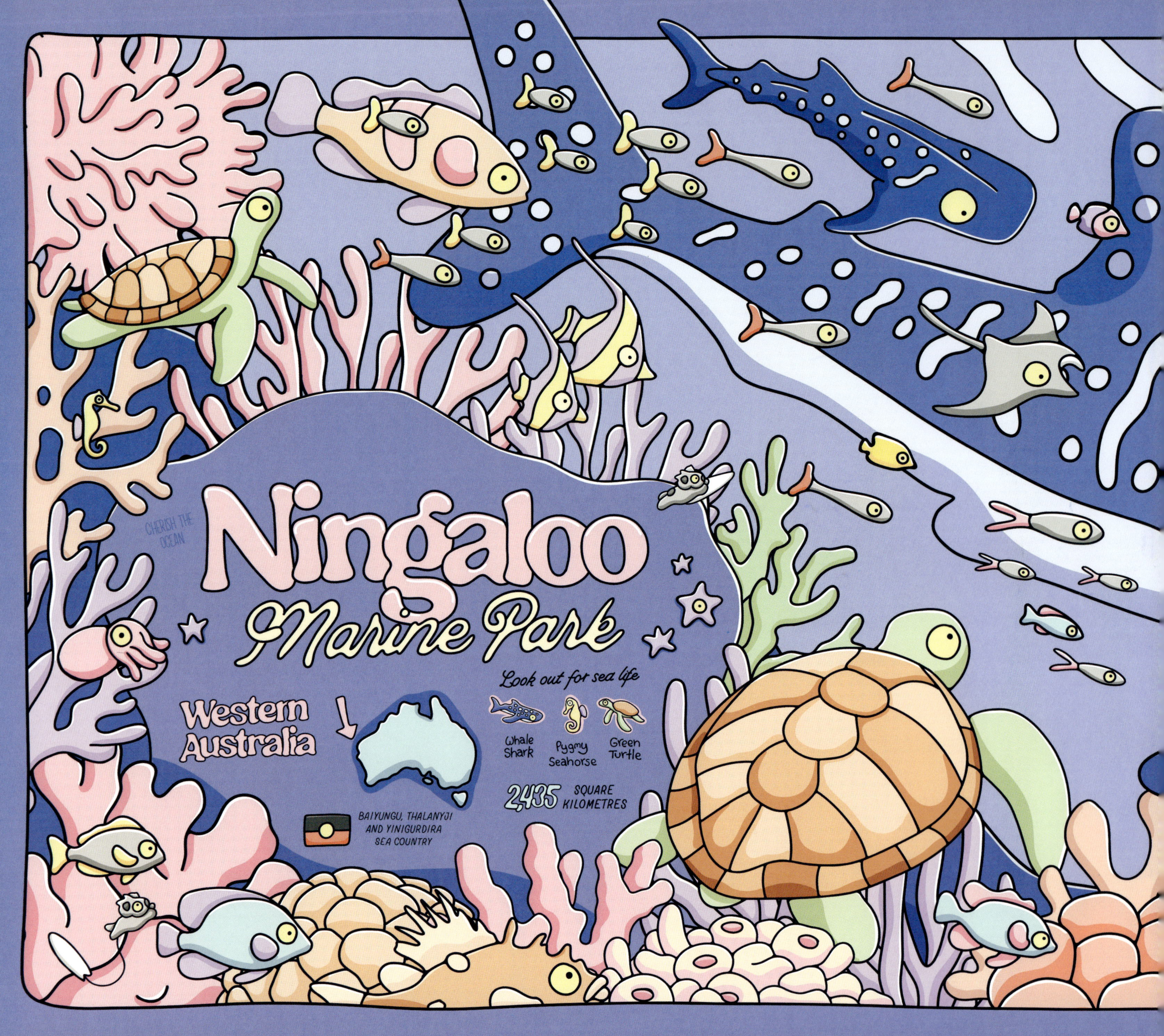
CHERISH THE OCEAN
Ningaloo
Marine Park
Western Australia
Look out for sea life
Whale Shark
Pygmy Seahorse
Green Turtle
2,435 SQUARE KILOMETRES
BAIYUNGU, THALANYJI AND YINIGURDIRA SEA COUNTRY

Ningaloo Marine Park is Australia's longest
fringing barrier reef, attracting over 400
Whale Sharks who swim here to fill their
bellies with plankton. Did you know Whale
Sharks are not actually whales or sharks?
They're the world's largest fish!

Ningaloo
Marine Park
Uluru-Kata Tjuta
NATIONAL PARK
Purnululu
National Park
Western
Australia
South
Australia
Great
Australian
Bight
Marine
Park

Gulf Of Carpentaria
MARINE PARK
Daintree
National Park
CORAL SEA
MARINE PARK
Northern Territory
QUEENSLAND
HANDA-
EYRE
Park
BLUE MOUNTAINS
National Park
NEW SOUTH WALES
Lord Howe Island
Marine Park
ACT
GRAMPIANS
National Park
Victoria
RICKETTS POINT
MARINE SANCTUARY
TASMANIA
CRADLE MOUNTAIN-
LAKE ST CLAIR
National Park
HUON
Marine Park